KV-193-038

This book belongs to:

.................................................

Retold by Gaby Goldsack

Illustrated by Emma Lake

Language consultants: Betty Root and Monica Hughes

This edition published by Parragon in 2009

Parragon
Chartist House
15-17 Trim Street
Bath BA1 1HA, UK
www.parragon.com

Copyright © Parragon Books Ltd 2002

All rights reserved. No part of this publication may be reproduced, stored in a retrieval system, or transmitted by any means, mechanical, photocopying, recording or otherwise, without the prior permission of the copyright holder.

ISBN 978-1-4054-8708-5
Printed in China

# Sleeping Beauty

# PaRragon

Bath New York Singapore Hong Kong Cologne Delhi Melbourne

# Notes for Parents

These **Gold Stars**® reading books encourage and support children who are learning to read.

## Starting to read

• Start by reading the book aloud to your child. Take time to talk about the pictures. They often give clues about the story. The easy-to-read speech bubbles provide an excellent 'joining-in' activity.

• Over time, try to read the same book several times. Gradually your child will want to read the book aloud with you. It helps to run your finger under the words as you say them.

• Occasionally, stop and encourage your child to continue reading aloud without you. Join in again when your child needs help.

This is the next step towards helping your child become an independent reader.

• Finally, your child will be ready to read alone. Listen carefully and give plenty of praise. Remember to make reading an enjoyable experience.

## Using your stickers

The fun colour stickers in the centre of the book and fold-out scene board at the back will help your child re-enact parts of the story, again and again.

## Remember these four stages:

• Read the story **to** your child.

• Read the story **with** your child.

• Encourage your child to read **to you**.

• Listen to your child read **alone**.

Long ago a king and queen wanted a baby.

One day their dream came true.

They had a baby girl. She was lovely.

The king and queen were happy.

"Everyone in the land must see the new princess," said the queen.

"We must have a party," said the king.

We must have a party.

Everyone in the land came to the party.

Four good fairies came to see the new princess.

They waved their wands. They cast their spells.

*She will be beautiful.*

"She will be beautiful,"
said the first.

*She will be wise.*

"She will be wise," said the second.

*She will be kind.*

"She will be kind,"
said the third.

Just then there was a puff of smoke.

It was the wicked fairy.

How dare you forget me.

"How dare you forget to invite me!"

cried the wicked fairy.

The king and queen had forgotten to invite her.

We forgot!

The wicked fairy waved her wand.
She cast a wicked spell.

"The princess will prick her finger
on a spinning wheel and die!" she cried.

She will prick her finger and die!

14

There was a puff of smoke.

The wicked fairy disappeared.

The king and queen were sad.

The fourth fairy waved her wand.

"I cannot break the wicked spell,"
she said. "But I can change it.
When the princess pricks her finger she will
not die. She will sleep for one hundred years.
A kiss from a prince will wake her."